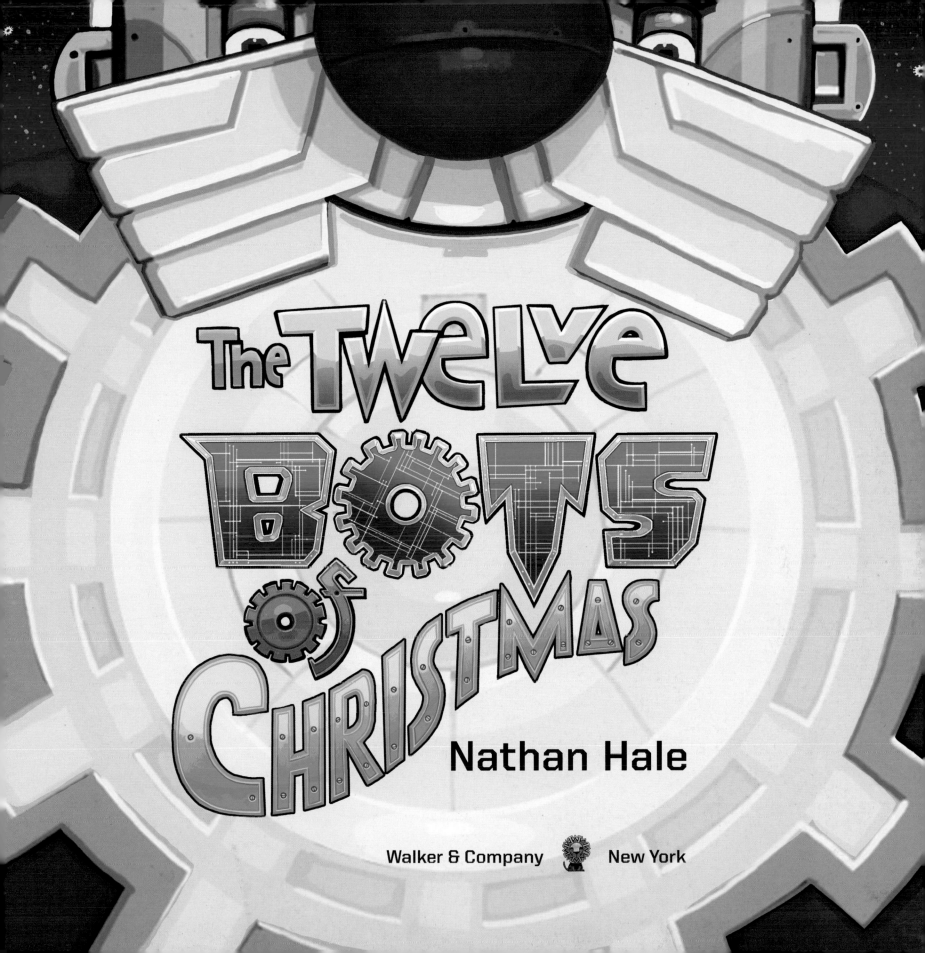

The Twelve Bots of Christmas

Nathan Hale

Walker & Company   New York

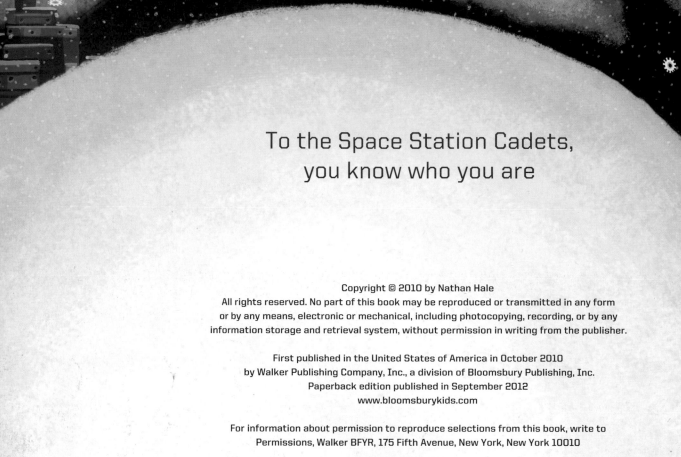

To the Space Station Cadets,
you know who you are

First published in the United States of America in October 2010
by Walker Publishing Company, Inc., a division of Bloomsbury Publishing, Inc.
Paperback edition published in September 2012
www.bloomsburykids.com

For information about permission to reproduce selections from this book, write to
Permissions, Walker BFYR, 175 Fifth Avenue, New York, New York 10010

The Library of Congress has cataloged the hardcover edition as follows:
Hale, Nathan.
The twelve bots of Christmas / Nathan Hale — 1st U.S. ed.
p.   cm.
Summary: In this variation on the folk song "The Twelve Days of Christmas," Robo-Santa gives gifts that
consist of electronic gear, including a cartridge in a gear tree, three wrench hens, and nine droids a-dancing.
ISBN 978-0-8027-2237-9 (hardcover) · ISBN 978-0-8027-2238-6 (reinforced)
1. Children's songs—United States. 2. Christmas music—Texts.
[1. Robots—Songs and music. 2. Christmas—Songs and music. 3. Christmas music. 4. Songs.] I. Title.
PZ8.3.H135Tw 2010   782.42–dc22   [E]   2010009541

ISBN 978-0-8027-3399-3 (paperback)

Art created digitally using Photoshop on a Wacom CINTIQ monitor
Typeset in United Sans Regular
Book design by Nathan Hale and Donna Mark

Printed in China by Hung Hing Printing (China) Co., Ltd., Shenzhen, Guangdong
1 3 5 7 9 10 8 6 4 2

On the first day of Christmas,
Robo-Santa gave to me . . .

... a Cartridge in a Gear Tree!

On the second day of Christmas,
Robo-Santa gave to me . . .

**Two Turbo-Doves
and a Cartridge in a Gear Tree!**

On the third day of Christmas,
Robo-Santa gave to me . . .

**Three Wrench Hens,
Two Turbo-Doves,
and a Cartridge in a Gear Tree!**

On the fourth day of Christmas,
Robo-Santa gave to me . . .

Four Calling Borgs,
Three Wrench Hens,
Two Turbo-Doves,
and a Cartridge in a Gear Tree!

On the fifth day of Christmas,
Robo-Santa gave to me . . .

FIVE BOT.

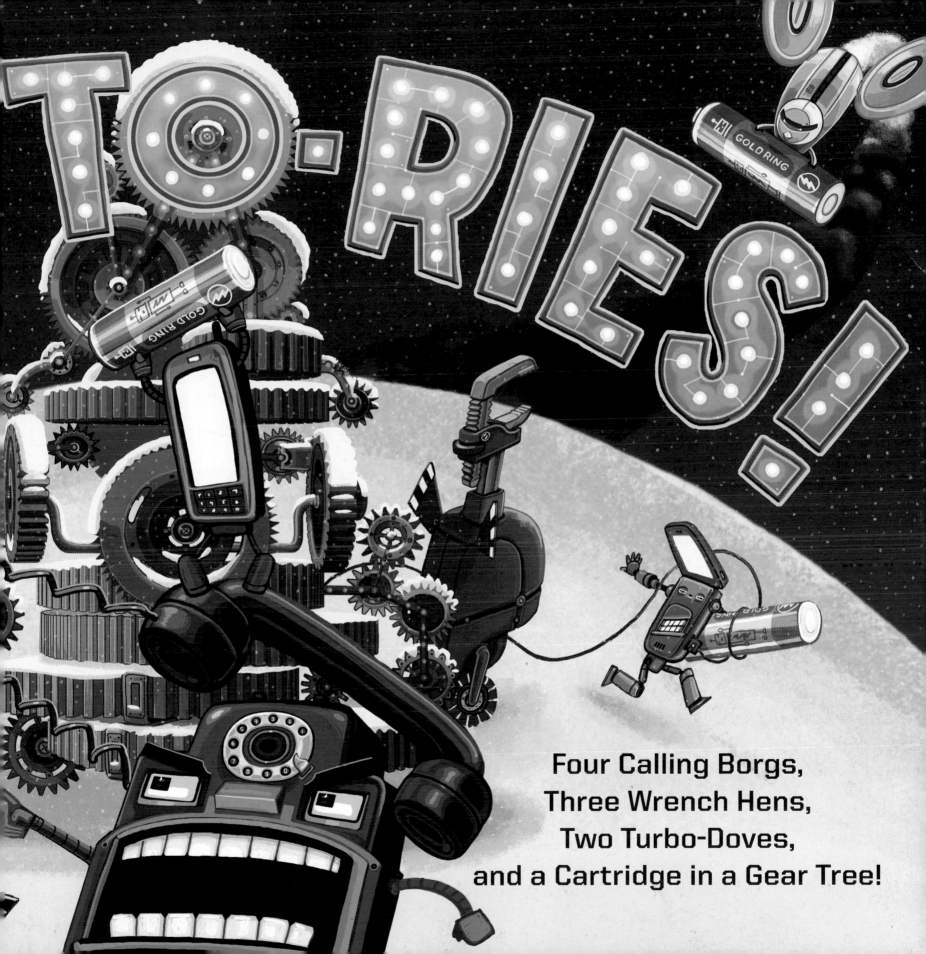

On the sixth day of Christmas,
Robo-Santa gave to me . . .

Six Geese-o-Matics,
FIVE BOT-TO-RIES!
Four Calling Borgs,
Three Wrench Hens,
Two Turbo-Doves,
and a Cartridge in a Gear Tree!

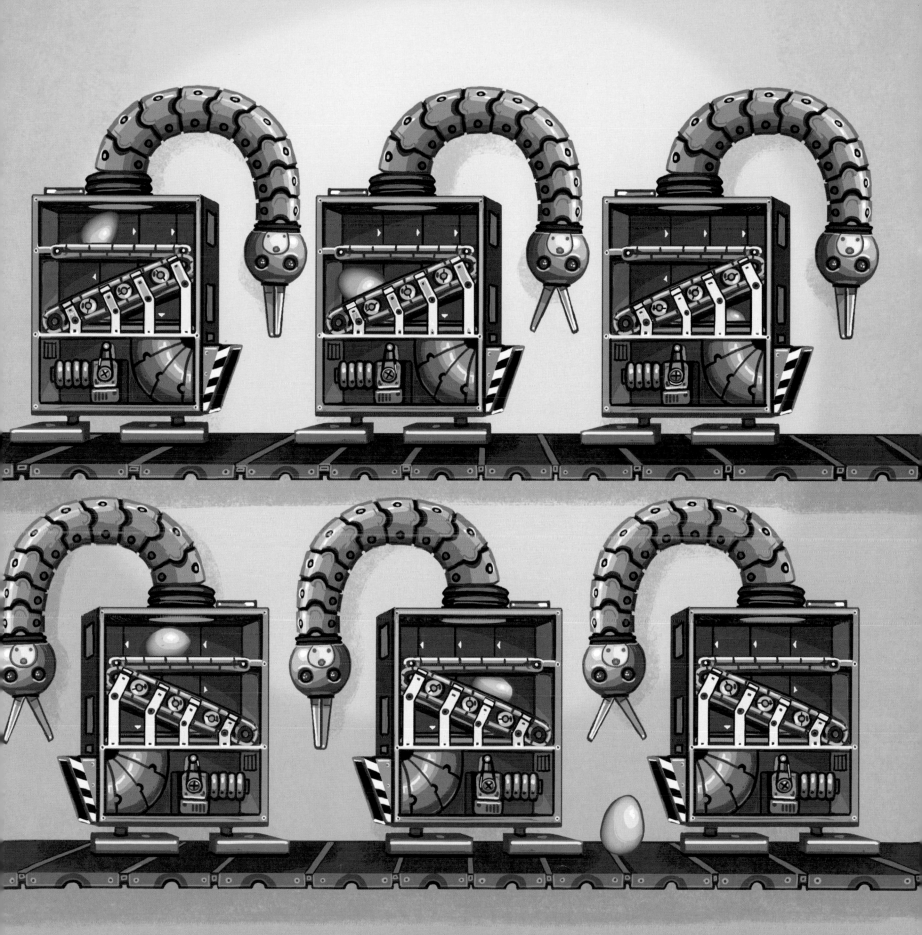

On the seventh day of Christmas,
Robo-Santa gave to me . . .

Seven Sub-Trons swimming,
Six Geese-o-Matics,
FIVE BOT-TO-RIES!
Four Calling Borgs,
Three Wrench Hens,
Two Turbo-Doves,
and a Cartridge in a Gear Tree!

On the eighth day of Christmas,
Robo-Santa gave to me . . .

Eight Moto-Milkers,
Seven Sub-Trons swimming,
Six Geese-o-Matics,
FIVE BOT-TO-RIES!
Four Calling Borgs,
Three Wrench Hens,
Two Turbo-Doves,
and a Cartridge in a Gear Tree!

On the ninth day of Christmas,
Robo-Santa gave to me . . .

Nine Droids a-dancing,
Eight Moto-Milkers,
Seven Sub-Trons swimming,
Six Geese-o-Matics,
FIVE BOT-TO-RIES!
Four Calling Borgs,
Three Wrench Hens,
Two Turbo-Doves,
and a Cartridge in a Gear Tree!

On the tenth day of Christmas,
Robo-Santa gave to me . . .

Ten Clock-Lords sleeping,
Nine Droids a-dancing,
Eight Moto-Milkers,
Seven Sub-Trons swimming,
Six Geese-o-Matics,
FIVE BOT-TO-RIES!
Four Calling Borgs,
Three Wrench Hens,
Two Turbo-Doves,
and a Cartridge in a Gear Tree!

On the eleventh day of Christmas,
Robo-Santa gave to me . . .

Eleven Techno-Pipers,
Ten Clock-Lords sleeping,
Nine Droids a-dancing,
Eight Moto-Milkers,
Seven Sub-Trons swimming,
Six Geese-o-Matics,
FIVE BOT-TO-RIES!
Four Calling Borgs,
Three Wrench Hens,
Two Turbo-Doves,
and a Cartridge in a Gear Tree!

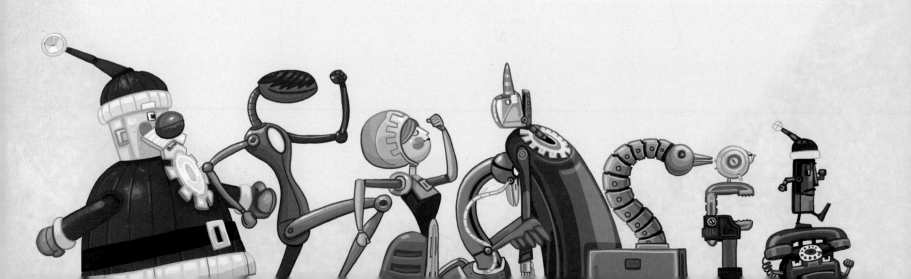

On the twelfth day of Christmas,
Robo-Santa gave to me . . .

Twelve Beat Bots thumping,
Eleven Techno-Pipers,
Ten Clock-Lords sleeping,
Nine Droids a-dancing,
Eight Moto-Milkers,
Seven Sub-Trons swimming,
Six Geese-o-Matics,
FIVE BOT-TO-RIES!
Four Calling Borgs,
Three Wrench Hens,
Two Turbo-Doves,
and a Cartridge in a Gear Tree!

Nathan Hale

has illustrated several books, including *The Dinosaurs' Night Before Christmas*, *Animal House*, and the graphic novel *Rapunzel's Revenge*. Since the gifts in the original "Twelve Days of Christmas" are ones that most kids wouldn't want, Nathan decided that robots would make a much better story than birds and dancing people. He thinks everyone should participate in the giving and receiving of robots during the holidays. Visit www.spacestationnathan.com to learn more about Nathan and to see his weekday Web comic.